T3-BUL-189

HONKER VISITS THE ISLAND

To my grandchildren
Gary, Andy, Mark, Kathy, Jackie
and Johnny

Honker Visits the Island

By Doris Van Liew Foster

Illustrated by Kurt Werth

LOTHROP, LEE & SHEPARD CO., INC.

NEW YORK

A long time ago many things happened
to the earth about us...
In this place the earth was rolled out
into sandy plains.
Here the cowboy rides his pony.
Listen to the song he sings:

"Away, away o'er the plains so free,
The cactus grows tall but it can't stop me,
It can't stop me, me, meeeeeee!"

In another place the earth was piled high,
then higher and higher until it was a
mountain stretching toward the sky.

Here the black bear roams alone.

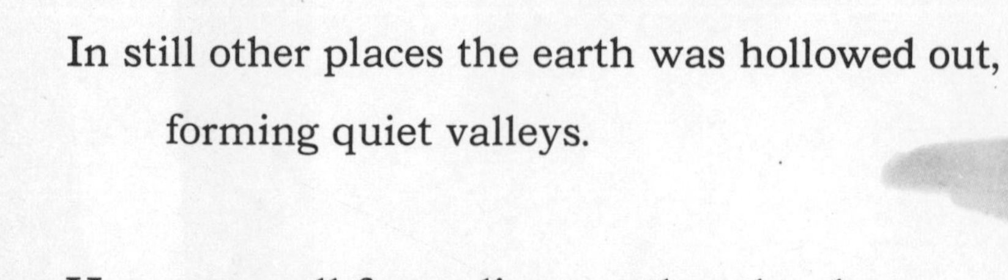

In still other places the earth was hollowed out,
forming quiet valleys.

Here on small farms live together the sheep,
the pig and friendly cow...
Count them in the meadow now.

But in only one place, just one,
was the earth raised from the waters
in the shape of a hand.

Now this hand held many lakes in its palm.
More blue than the sky above them.
And on one little lake,
was a tiny green cap of an island.

To this island one day came a man
who had been wandering about with his dog.
"This will be our home," decided the man,
gently patting his dog.

The man's name was Michigan Sam
and his dog was called Bowser.

Here Michigan Sam fished in the waters around
the island
catching bluegills, yellow perch, and spotted sunfish...

While on the island Bowser chased the chipmunks
from birch tree to birch tree...
But he never managed to catch one.

On a certain night in the spring of the year,
and seen only by a pale wispy moon,
a flying wedge of geese on their way north
stopped to rest one April night.

And that is when Honker came to live for a
time on the island.

When Michigan Sam saw Honker the following morning
he said, "I thought that I heard some wild geese
last night. You are a handsome fellow, Honker."
To Bowser, who was barking loudly
showing that he did not like this new visitor
Michigan Sam said, "Quiet Bowser, there is room
on the island for us all.
When Honker is ready he will leave."

The spring days turned to warm summer days,
but Honker seemed in no hurry to leave the island.

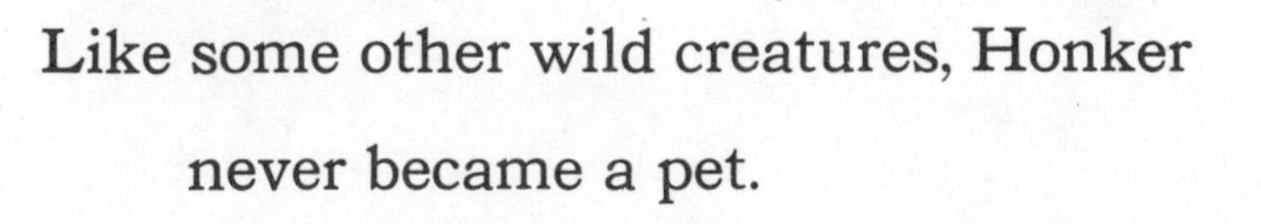

Like some other wild creatures, Honker
never became a pet.
Although Michigan Sam spoke gently to him each day,
Honker stayed out of reach, content to swim by
himself and watch from a distance.

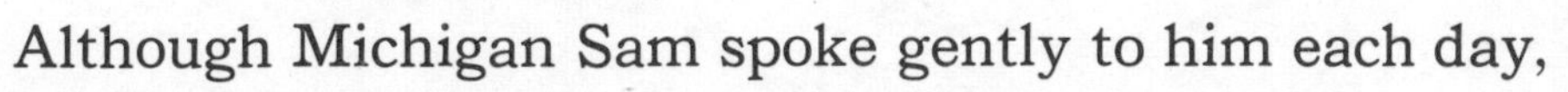

The day came when the hand held the harvest
gathered from the farmlands in the valley—
golden corn, purple grapes, and apples from the
orchard.

The sheep, the pig and the friendly cow
left the meadows to stay close in the
barnyard now.

Then on a certain night in the fall of the year,
and seen only by the full harvest moon,
a flying wedge of geese on their way south
stopped to rest one autumn night.

And that is when Honker said goodbye to the island.

The following morning, finding him gone,
Michigan Sam said to Bowser:
"I heard some wild geese last night.
I guess Honker went south with them; he was ready.
It was time too, for winter will be flying in
most any day now."

And so it was.
Soon snowflakes like soft white feathers
swirled out from the plains
and filled the valleys.

Michigan Sam spent the winter days
fishing through a hole in the ice,
while lazy Bowser dozed before an
open fire in the cottage...

and dreamed about Honker, the visitor who
came to live for a time on the island.

And a silvery winter moon looked down
to see the earth that is shaped
like a hand
wearing a snow-white mitten for winter.